Lovingly Dedicated...

*To the muse who leads me
into dark temptation.*

*And always and forever,
to Wendy.*

RUMORS OF VAMPIRES

4

RUMORS OF VAMPIRES

DODGY POEMS
& BLASPHEMOUS PRAYERS

BY

DELLA VAN HISE

EYE SCRY PUBLICATIONS

1

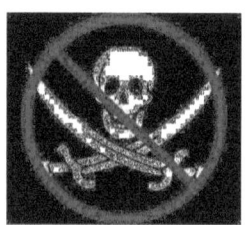

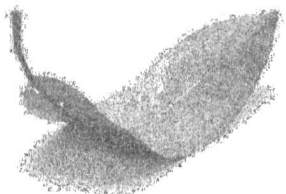

Rumors of Vampires

THE MUSE'S TWISTED KISS
AN INTRODUCTION

Poetry is a language unto itself - and one in which I don't consider myself anywhere near fluent. At best, I am a dabbler and a babbler at the edge of the pond, mainly interested in capturing a moment the same way a photographer might capture a fleeting image otherwise lost to the ages.

I'm okay with that - this sense that we are incredible yet insignificant beings moving through some inexplicable milieu of experience and emotion, longing and loss, love and grief. And yet, at the same time I'm not okay with it at all - for it is human nature to crave that which remains out of reach.

It is human nature to chase the muse that whispers midnight promises of eternity, but delivers cemeteries and funeral processions when the sun rises on another mundane day. It is human nature to want to live forever, even (and perhaps *especially*) if that promise were to be delivered in the form of an erotic if twisted kiss of eternal damnation and eternal salvation all wrapped up together in a vampire's embrace.

The vampire has been a mysterious and recurring icon in our human imaginings for as far back as anyone can determine. Some say it's only a myth. Others insist all myths have some basis in reality. A rare few of us choose to believe in vampires and faeries and alien visitors above and beyond any dull human-spawned deity. And such is the language of poetry - a way to explore our darkest fantasies and most forbidden desires without automatically being consigned to the psychiatrist's lumpy couch.

Some would say I suffer from depression. I would argue that I suffer from clarity, but also from the dark but beneficial curse of allowing myself to believe there is more to this world than we have been programmed to believe. It's not just what I *want* to believe. It's what I *have* to believe, or run the high risk of becoming just one more cog in the grinding machine that digests our imagination and craps it all out as rhetoric, pabulum and dogma. On the day I become that, I will shut down the computer and throw away my writing quill forever.

This particular collection of poetry may well be my last, and so I have thrown in some ancient scribblings as well as some new ones. Some of the offerings here come from my old and obscure chap books, most of which were only give-aways to friends and unsuspecting relatives. Those would include *The Dark Evolution, Conjuring the Vampyre, Paintings on the Devil's Inner Eye, Sundance & Other Ghost Towns That Never Were,* and *The Haunted Places.* I've tried not to include poems that were in *The Effect of Moonlight on Tombstone,* but on the off chance I overlooked something... so it goes when the eyes are tired and the glasses among the missing.

When I say this may be my last collection of poetry, it's not because I have any thoughts of leaving the planet anytime soon - though with my health conditions, that's definitely a possibility. I simply cannot predict what the future holds with regard to my writing, particularly in this new and insane age of internet and indie publishing, both of which have contributed to the disappearance (hopefully temporary) of my lifelong muse. He sends notes from time to time, telling me he's off in India or Australia or in my own back yard, always harvesting words and moments like grapes plucked to create the best wine. I am trying to believe him, but as all writers know, muses are fickle fuckers who have their own agendas and cooperate only when their own muse moves them.

For now, I hope you will enjoy *Rumors of Vampires*, and that it will bring you some measure of entertainment, a chill or two, or - if I've done my job - a stray thought to chase through the candlelit cathedral at the edge of Vampyreland.

Eternally, unconditionally,
Della Van Hise
November, 2017

Memorial Service

I plant wildflowers
on your grave,
Knowing
your coffin
lies empty.

SACRIFICE

The altar sizzles
whispering your name in smoke.
Vampires gather at the door,
reading meaning into my blood sacrifice:
      red coins scattered over dead flowers,
      broken crystals,
      a gargoyle's granite lips.

FORBIDDEN FRUIT

I hold in my hand
the night that never ends,
magick encased within reality's rind.
Peeling away the dayshine layers
one at a time,
I reveal the obsidian core
of my chosen damnation.

AFTERLIFE

Your ghost made love to me last night,
a pale shadowy thing that had your face.
It came to my door about midnight,
scratching at the screen like a lost pup.
When I led it to the kitchen for coffee,
it grabbed me with transparent hands,
telling me in your voice
"Love is a weakness of mortal flesh."
It sat me down in the chair
and said you were gone,
dead in a New York street
with snow melting like tears on your eyes.
It accused me of letting you go,
of failing to remind you of mortality.
It said you believed you'd live forever,
that bullets were only props
and cities hallucinations on a map.
It ranted and it howled,
throwing books off the shelves
and weeping like an orphan boy.
And when it was finished,
it left through an open window,
spreading itself over the clouds like mist
until fog settled deep in this valley.
I think this is what you've been wanting
since the moment of your conception:
tempting Death like a coiled serpent,
coming alive only when love
could no longer touch you.

UNFINISHED SYMPHONY

Somewhere on the side of this narrow road
a wind chime sings off-key,
but because some of the pieces are missing
the world we live in is only half finished.

In Vampyreland

The confessional is made of skulls
in the vampire cathedral
and the priest drinks his own blood,
unholy communion.
The greatest sin
is not to sin.

*

In Vampyreland,
power lines are bloodlines
and streets are arteries
filled with dark philosophy.
Shamans dispense starlight and magick
and pharmacies are filled with poetry
about the ancient myth of sunrise.

*

My heart is glass,
your words a hammer.
I want a crystal cherry
full of immortal blood.

PAPER CUT

You are memories sketched on rice paper,
alabaster phantom of sagebrush yesterdays,
never aging
forever as you were
that night in a May apart from Time,
when a few words you spoke
changed my mind
and severed my lifeline
for all eternity.

Today I saw my rag doll ghost
walking along the road
where you tossed this crappy poem
out the window of your Jeep
ten years ago or more
so I could find it on this December wind
and cut my wrist on its jagged edge,
tearing my world in two all over again.

STILL LIFE

Lightning takes a snapshot of the night:
      dying trees and trembling leaves,
      rain frozen in freefall,
      glittering stones littering desert floor,
      the vampire on the porch swing.

Old Woman Springs Road at Dawn

The hitchhiker waltzes with a red gas can
while a raven sings his awkward aria
to the dawn
and beats his wings
to fan the fires of the sun
and sound the temple chimes in Tibet
a hundred years
before any of us were born.
Phantoms fade in the rearview mirror
on dusty desert highways
where mirages come out to play.

SOLSTICE SACRAMENT

I prick my ring finger,
vein leading straight to the heart,
to leave a trail of red-crumbs
leading straight to my door.
I prey you follow me home.
I prey you are hungry.

INGREDIENTS

Fairy dust is largely comprised
   of mushroom spores and falling stars,
   the inner eye of the black angel's tears.
The vampire king haunts toadstool rings,
   admiring his reflection
   in drops of condensation
   gathering on the widow's web
   of my dreaming.

RELICS

Your tears are snowflakes,
silent crystals shed at night,
visible only in the misted bloom
of lonesome yellow streetlamps.
I thought I heard an angel crying,
but it was only rusted chimes
scratching at the wind.
I stand in an open doorway,
counting lost dreams blowing past me,
bitter relics of other men's sleep.

Toxin

Your love is toxic
yet I hold you
pressed like poison ivy
between the pages
of my fatal mortality.
One day
the venom will end us both.

ECHOES

Shadow men converge
at the round table of sentient silence,
drinking a toast of witch's venom
and disturbing echoes
left behind by a passing train.

When I asked the vampire
where he came from,
all he said was this:
"I reside at the edge of the world,
at the end of time."

The Footfalls of Vampires

In this room where perpetual winter dwells,
I listen for the footfalls of vampires,
most often found
in the flutter of moth wings,
delicate imprints in the dust
where spiders pace the windowsill;
in the hush of locust blossoms
pushed on a broom of straw-scented wind
across the desert floor.
You thrive on candle breath
and the shivers of children
who still *see* the tender zephyr
pulling the curtain aside
is really your lace-gloved hand
caressing the pale neck
of this moon-dappled midnight.
On my altar a burning skull keeps vigil,
casting hieroglyph shadows like rune bones
on a world of tombstones.
Time is running backward,
softly counter-clockwise.
Such are the footfalls of vampires.

Threads

The mortal world is sewn together
with obligations and words and watches,
linear threads thru time,
leading to dust, to the grave.
Vampyreland is bound
by webs of pure perception,
crazy glue of truth beyond reason,
embracing intuition
we can only call
magick.

DEAD END

Some place
at the crossroads
of Sundance and Nightfall,
you stand waiting for me
with secrets in your eyes
and rain in your pockets.

After all these turns,
all these paths leading
from Nowhere to Netherwhen
and back again,
I ultimately see a wicked truth:
   I cannot get There
   from Here.

DOLL HOUSES

It's another ghost town
lost along the road to Nowhere
like broken legos
strewn over derelict attic.
Signs with missing letters,
faded and bent,
point the way to train stations
and graveyards
and eternal salvation
while Time sits on the side of the highway,
scratching the paint off the doll houses,
carving his name into aging mortal faces,
waiting for the dust to settle
in his slaughterhouse hands.

UNDERTAKER

Man is only a machine,
his sole soul function
to be a gravedigger
at his life-long funeral procession
of petty dramas and clichés.

MAINTENANCE NOTE

Something keeps tripping
the motion sensor
and making the sun come up.
This needs to be fixed.
Moonlight and candles
are quite sufficient.

SHAPE SHIFTER

Time assumes the shape of a coyote,
creeping close to the fire
to hear the sound of my breathing.
I cut my wrist
on the sharp edge of the moon,
feeding drops of blood
to the trickster,
red coins to pay the ferryman
for passage back home.

VISION QUEST

Firefly pumpkin eyes
open on the mortal world,
blink each Halloween.

ANSWERING MACHINE

You've reached a place
where it is always October,
where witches cast spells
and summon shadows
and vampires are honored guests.
So leave a message if you dare.
Something will get back to you
when you least expect it.

IMMORTAL GARDENER

Vampires plant dead trees
at the edges of cemeteries -
   skeletal sentinels,
   sycamore and poplar
   with outstretched limbs
   upon which are hung
   the fruits of forbidden Truth.
I pluck an invisible mushroom
and wash it down with blood,
choosing the sanction of shadows,
the pentacle over the cross,
evolution in the absence of grace.
Long live the dead tree
at the end of Eden.

MESSAGE FROM THE FAR SIDE OF THE BRIDGE

The twin dances naked in the dark,
immortal me
with rounded earth goddess body
wrapped in a cape of long dark hair.
Frenzied shaman priestess,
pregnant with the night that never ends,
pendulous breasts full of magick.
Spinning near, she whispers,
        "Voodoo is the answer,"
a voice from the far side of a quantum leap,
the future speaking to the past,
passing secrets in an alpha flash dream.
That she exists must mean I listened.

The Vampire Cathedral

Snow comes,
pale cold blood of dangerous angels
falling to silence this night.
The vampire cathedral reveals itself at last,
with steeples of ice,
minarets of bone,
altars of shattered glass.
Its belfries house broken hearts,
unbeating,
still as 3 a.m.

TRANSIENT TRAVELERS

Life is a fragile trick
carried on the tip
of the harlequin's walking stick.
The bells on his cap are skulls,
hollow souvenirs
vacated by hermit crab souls.

SHADOW PUPPETS

The hand of God
makes shadow puppets in the sun,
women and men enacting illusory lives,
phantoms at the mercy
of a merciless toy maker.

I am a different sort of shadow,
thrown by a vampire's candle,
projected against the obsidian screen
of a Life that never ends.

Let the stars fall.
Let the moon fail.
My creator casts me in wax,
a thing outside of time,
on the wrong side of God.

POST MORTEM

I wrote down all the answers
in a book of matches
but it got tossed out in an old coat pocket
six months after I died,
just one more thrift store jacket
going nowhere in the middle of summer.
So now I'm counting ghosts,
some of them yours, some of them mine,
loitering on the skid row outskirts of time.
Sometimes I see them dancing,
hear them singing,
feel them screaming,
just phantoms of who we were back then,
characters in a recurring dream.

CONCLUSION

Death is a poison arrow
shot by God
into the heart of Man.
Vampires are the antidote.
Should good and evil
god and devil
not now be redefined?

TIME

Death creates itself,
given time.

MINDFUL SHADOW

I-Am the dream,
wraith shadow in starshine
whisperer of sentient gnosis.

VAMPIRE HEAVEN ON EARTH

If there is a heaven
surely it hides behind storm clouds
and dead trees.
Its sun is a black candle
lit by a witch,
its patron saint a pirate,
its flagship the *Marie Celeste*
where faeries still gather
to tell tall tales on the bow.
Its Creator is Greek
and has fang teeth
where the faithful are impaled:
their eternal torment,
their eternal reward.

With wicked fang teeth
the marionette severs her strings,
dancing free of puppeteers and playwrights
through the landscape of vampire dreams
and worlds without end.

"Free," she cries,
a wild bird singing without realizing
it's just the lines called for
in the mortal script
that preaches free will,
never really allowing it.

QUANTUM KISS

All ravens are sorcerers
in service to the King of Spades
in a land where Forever
is a cool winter season
and Infinity only an intersection
where Magic and Logic cross swords
in a quantum kiss that never ends.
The blood in my chalice is warm,
ink for the time-keeper's quill.

All the Lost and Shiny Pieces

Fragments gather round the fire,
starship captain fantasies
conversing with the ghosts
of martial arts masters
and the little blond girl
who never grew up
so she would never have to die.

The vampire king drinks gently
from each tributary,
mingling the blood of fragmented selves
in immortal veins
until all the pieces are whole again.

IN THE BETWEEN

Beneath the frozen lake
the world of matter and men
lies in the arms of Time and Ruin.
Walking on water
is best done in winter,
in between the Now and the Zen.

SEASONS OF ASH

Early autumn
when hearts already brittle
  break
scattering the ashes of old pets
and older dreams
lost in the hip pocket
of Time.

CONTRACT

The night is full
with promises of rain,
contracts on the wind,
signed by rusted chimes.

STATEMENT

Raven wings dust darkness aside,
blushing the sky with dawn.
The shaman haunts adobe ruins,
seeking ghosts of old miners
to ask their counsel on life and death.
October wind blows cold yellow daylight,
whispering with certainty
that all the spirits are dead,
their only afterlife
a dim and fading reflection
in the mirrored memories
of migrating mortals.

Nearby, stones spell out a message,
black rock on pale sand:
                    I AM.

MANIFESTATIONS

My fireplace opens into the underworld,
where pallid ashes of last week's magick
stir firestorms in the hearts
of gargoyles.
Bleached bones assemble as men
and drink a toast of tears
from a bend in the River Styx,
chasing harlequin dreams
that follow vapor trails of curling smoke
back to this haunted room.

Little Girl Lost

Lost boys paint the sky
with a wide brush
the color of dried blood,
deep scarlet scratches
on the face of Mother Dusk.
Leaves on the locust tree
are whispering again,
writing messages in the sand
with alphabets of spent blooms
cut away by the sharp silver blade
of a sliver crescent moon.
In this casket of organic matter,
I fall through time,
counting comets and past autumns
on a broken abacus
lost in August of '69.
The girl I was back then
shakes her fist at the night,
begging me to break the clock,
hold back the dust.
The same stars shone
in the same bright sky,
but closer somehow then,
closer then than now.

AWARENESS

I am not the reflection in the mirror
nor the one who stands
before the looking glass.
I am instead the space between,
nothing but an idea of Being.

DEFLOWERING

The shadows have sharp edges tonight,
jagged cookie cut-outs
splintering the delicate hymen
between your world and mine.

BLANKET

I sleep in a tapestry
of tangled stars
thrown down over the earth
to keep the dreams of old men
from escaping.

COMFORT ZONES

If you made love to me
perhaps the solidity
of your preternatural body
would fill this void of emptiness.

Night is bending the sky
back to black
where such thoughts are no longer safe.

Bring me to Life
    through the portal of mortal death.

If I believed you'd do it
there would be no sanctuary safe enough.

Please.
Give me reason to believe.

UNHOLY COMMUNION

Your blood stretching my veins,
moving inside my heart,
a cold but perfect beating
as a man's pulse of passion spending
or raven's wing on winter's dusk.
I drink your wine
from ceremonial chalice,
sliding my tongue over splintered lip
so we may lie together in perfect incest.

MARK OF THE BEAST

It's half-past November
in the season of storms.
On the thorn of a dead rose
I prick my finger,
this flow of blood
the only evidence of life.
But if I bled to death
it could not erase you from my veins,
the stain on my mortal heart.

Autumn Valentines

Autumn valentines
have broken hearts
black and orange, never pink.
I write you love letters
on yellow leaves,
setting them free at dusk.

Candy corns line the nests of brownies,
who only breed in uneven Octobers.
If you were to devour me,
I would consider it a fine
if fatal
gift.

GARGOYLE

Lonesome stone gargoyle
whose hematite heart is larger
than most mortal men's.
Some nights I hear him weeping
for fallen doves and souls lost at sea.

Eternal Elixir

In the shadow of a sepulcher
bearing my name,
I wear the night as a second skin,
playing Time like a grand piano.
From the slashed wrists
of things that do not exist,
I drink myself into being -
   the ghost inside the machine.

Receptacles

Pumpkins thrive
at the cemetery's edge,
hollow heartless receptacles
holding the dreams
of the dead.

BETTER DAYS

When *The Ship Song* played spontaneously
in the middle of the night
and books and rocks and broken clocks
were found stacked in empty rooms
where shadows held audience
with wandering vampires
who came to dine on old memories
trapped in black & white photographs...

When time stopped at 3:38 a.m.
and we Dreamed together
of crumbling skyscrapers
and dead poets writing lyrics in stardust
for the crickets to sing...

When we danced together on desert hilltops,
damning the dawn
and pretending the rags we wore
were tuxedoes and magickal gowns...

"Those were the days," her heart murmurs.
"Those were better days."

The Dreamer & the Dreamed

Asleep in a bed of leaves
beneath a bone-naked tree
growing on the shore of Styx,
the vampire king Dreams me into being,
a pallid mortal night mare
struggling to become the Dreamer again.

Guardians

Gargoyles guard the crypt,
keeping the curious away,
concealing the darkest secret:
   my grave is empty.

STORM

Outside my window
the street turns to a river
sweeping sticks and stones
and dried bones
to their new home.
Some place else.
Nowhere special.
The world rearranges itself in a storm,
tired of the same old view.
Coyote voices sketch revised maps
on wet black canvas.

THE TAO

It has to be real.
You.
Me.
Immortal eternity.
I am the shadow
thrown by 13 candles,
whole only in the night,
the tao of dusk
written in blood
on the far side of the bridge
not yet built.

PARANORMAL ACTIVITY

Make the lights flicker,
cause the foyer to chill
and let the planchette
go sailing on the cold spot
in the doubting part of my heart.

I need to believe, you see
and so I ask these tasks -
not because I don't believe in you,
but because I need to re-believe
in me.

WILD RIDE

Hobby horse shadows gallop the sand,
broken free
from the carousel clock face of time,
driven by the whip of unforgiving wind.
Moonglow bleaches the night grey-white
and on the jagged mountain horizon
a rainbow comes and goes,
there, then gone,
eyeliner on the faces of angels
who shed falling stars like feathers.

DESK CLERK

There's a hotel in the abyss
with red velvet curtains trimmed in gold
and all the coffee tables
are broken windshields.
The only access
is through the labyrinthine corridor
of shamanic visions, woeful dreams.
You wait at the front desk of Neverland,
tall thin fiend in a ragged tux.
I bring you wild lavender
and fireplace ashes,
my insignificant offering
to the landlord of eternity.

CREATION

Your sheets bear the scars
of our love, our lust:
candle wax on black satin,
lamp oil stains of the ritual,
a hair on your pillow,
shed in passion,
drops of my blood,
spilled to feed your immortal hunger
and create my own.

THE MUSE

Sheer black drape
lifts on this ghostly wind
in this haunted house.
Spirits of impending winter
chase little girls into old women,
young boys into bitter old men.

I followed a dream
out the window and down the street,
but when I caught up to it,
it was behind me,
off following itself through the desert again.
In a robe of purple velvet,
you conjure me
to the edge of the void,
luring me to jump,
willing me to fly.

LADY IN WAITING

The desert speaks in tongues,
language of silence,
paradigm of long shadows,
dead tree dwellers
only coming alive at dusk.
I haunt old mirrors,
waiting for a reflection
to show me who
I-Am.

ALL HALLOWS

Tonight I will put on the old clothes,
the ones with the indistinct scent
of faded cologne and chimney smoke.
Tonight the velvet cape will be my wings,
and the masks will all be shed.
Tonight... I will be me.
For this hallowed eve,
I will finally be free.

TELL-TALE SIGNS

Stained glass dragonflies
tell me you've been here again,
prowling the midnight,
admiring your shadow in my mirror.
The snapshots on the shelf
aren't where I left them,
slightly left or a little bit right
of where they were last night.
I was seventeen in that one,
twenty-six or seven in another,
a pale blonde witch at the edge
of the Salton Sea,
yesterday's bitch staring back at me.
I feel you watching me in the past,
vampire eyes gazing back in time
as easily as mortals peer thru windows.
Aching, I weep for faded days,
a crumbling rose, black as moonlight blood,
paper petals just pages
in time's diary of lies.
I dream, I scream:
  Take me thru the looking glass,
  into photographs past,
  through the red doorway of your veins,
  immortality's secret well.
Creep silently in my empty room,
but never write my name in dust.
The dragonflies will tell.

CROSSING OVER

In a land where autumn
does not patiently wait at the edge of town,
you stand in a field of Indian corn,
stroking a wild black kitten
like rubbing a genie's bottle.
Sparks ascend,
forming the stars,
just tiny night light eyes
of blind jack-o-lanterns.
I wait at the haunted train station,
counting ghosts in dusty windows.
Across the tracks,
dusk lord shadow come to life,
you beckon with crooked finger,
the promise of a fatal embrace
flickering in ayahuasca eyes.
How often have I started toward you,
only to shy away
from the oncoming train
which is the only entryway to your arms?
Safe in my deluded illusion of a safer world,
I dress in black
and court the shadows,
writing love songs to lostlings,
gathering the courage
to cross the tracks.

Mercy Killing

Cold wind blows the day away,
leaving only ashes of deepening dusk.
The vampire king skips
over gingerbread rooftops,
nibbling at the eaves and chimneys
of mortality
until the world mercifully disappears.

LENTICULAR SEPTEMBER

Autumn is restless,
waiting to hatch
from the heart
of summer's merciful death.

BIRTH PAINS

The shadows here are born wet –
  children of the night rains
  whose parents are iron lanterns
  and lightning strikes.

AFFAIR

The blood of Life
flows from the slashed wrist
of a deranged god
who created Time
to be the nagging bride
of Death himself.

DO NOT DISTURB

Do not disturb the dust.
It is sleeping.
Remembering
all the secrets told here
in this broken-hearted
purple sanctuary.

FICKLE

Even the stars,
patient immortal lovers,
fade and fall
if left too long alone.

HARD DRIVE

Time is a memory,
this diary the hard drive
where childhood and wolf songs are stored.
The machine counts its toes,
afraid of amnesia and clocks.

THE END OF AN ENDLESS ROAD

Here the picket fences are black,
fallen over with time,
covered with moss
at the edge of an unhallowed bone garden.

You dance to the arrhythmia
of a broken metronome,
conjuring immortals to manifest
at the end of an endless road
strewn with wayward pumpkins,
scattered with acorns.

The night breathes you into being,
an unsettled spirit
possessing my pen.

A PARADIGM OF SHADOWS

The night is cast
on a paradigm of shadows:
   coyote and wolf,
   owl and puma,
   prowling the cold spring dusk,
   just ghosts of altar smoke
   in the sorcerer's dream.

The chime in my garden
sings bamboo hymns,
summoning my lost soul,
expecting no answer.

Immortals skate thin ice
skimming the surface of Styx
on broomstick starships
bound for eternity.

OF DOLL HOUSES AND LOST ROADS

It's another ghost town
scattered along the road to nowhere
like broken legos strewn over dusty attic.
Signs with missing letters,
faded and cracked,
point the way
to train stations and graveyards
and houses of eternal salvation
while Time sits on the side of the highway,
scratching the paint off the doll houses,
carving his name into aging faces,
waiting for the dust to settle
in skeletal hands.

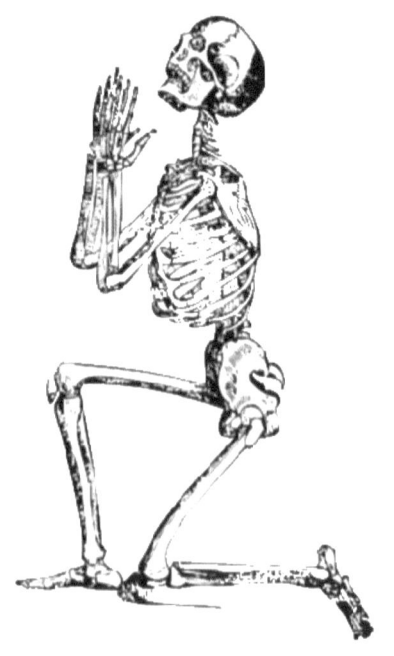

CHANT

It is you to whom I whisper
my darkest prayers:
    Make me real.
    Open my heart with a fang.
    Give me immortal birth and breath.

Vampire
Father
Incubus
Lover
    Come to me now
    Make me yours
    Forever.

MAPS & CLOCKS & WHISKEY BOTTLES

Spirits are whispering in the garden,
copper chime tongues chattering
metal lips murmuring messages
scripted in wind cipher.
The vampire king takes notes in red ink,
decoding the meaning
in scraps of poetry.
Beyond the final fragment of Time
on a map where clocks can't travel,
mermen frolic in whiskey bottles
filled with immortal elixir.

FOREPLAY

The autumn king
   is courting the crone again,
   tainting the wind with early apple scent,
   teasing the black river
   with caskets cast in the shapes of leaves,
   kissing the paned window
   with ejaculate of snow.

In the midnight realm,
   coyote songs have grown lonely,
   and bats are whispering
   of mysteries humans never see.

Death is grooming his winter brides,
   planning funerals like weddings,
   picking out fresh-cut coffins
   of cedar and mahogany and pine.

It's all just foreplay,
   the thunder before the storm,
   the dark before the dreams,
   the kiss before the dance.

OPEN DOOR

It is the season of silhouettes
sharp as paper edges,
the time for thinking of sunken ships
and honoring the locust trees
which will yield next year's broomsticks,
not ready for harvest until late October.
A whirligig made of old pie tins
stirs the air
to mix a potion of sagebrush
and dust from the wings of Monarchs
and displaced grains of sand
migrating on the wind.
Someone left the door open
to Vampyreland
and stained glass faeries
are oiling their wings with blood
and preening their hair with combs
gleaned from the bleached bones
of long-dead saints and martyrs.

IMMORTAL MEMORIES

Perhaps in a thousand years and some
    when Earth is only comet dust
    and all the humans have fled,
    we will dine on rocket soot
    and sapphire twilights...
    our only identities
    the muted memories
    of what we are
    and who we have been.

KITTENS

Nightshade and Hemlock
are the vampire's kittens,
black as moongone sky,
woven of pixie wing
and spidersilk
fed on the red red milk
from the flat male breast
of their immortal Maker.

The Fourth Floor

My dreams say you live
in an empty house with many rooms
and staircases everywhere,
some steep, some stone,
some marble, some glass,
leading up, always up
to a room where all the windows are broken
and sparrows chatter at dusk
on the haunted fourth floor
while you sit in the only chair
waiting for night to fall,
looking in, looking out
for a hint at which mortal doors
will open for you tonight.

MICROCOSM

The totality of the universe
is written in the last leaf
struggling to cling to the tree.
Too soon,
   the winds blow fierce,
   and that which was alive
   lives no more.
As above, so below.
As below,
forevermore.

NOTHING UNREAL EXISTS

Nothing unreal exists,
Therefore
I will believe in faeries
and sprites
and the curative magick
of a vampire's kiss.
After all
nothing unreal exists.

CONJURING THE VAMPIRE

My dreams bleed bougainvilleas,
crimson petals sweeping narrow streets
somewhere in Old Mexico.
The door before me bears lacy carnations,
picked from the gardens of the living
by the gloved hand of the vampire king.
"My teeth are sharp," you whisper,
          "sharp as the pain you crave."
The bed is red,
wet with my blood
spilled before you before I was born,
stored in this room in this dream,
waiting for me to find it again.
I drink in the scarlet dreamings,
bringing them back to my waking world,
magick elixir luring you to follow.

JUDGMENT

Beneath the city of Umberlight
where the Fractured River flows,
damned souls migrate to plead their case.

Testimony is heard by The Beast,
whispered into elfin ear
by the horned pet
in whose lap Death chooses to rest.

If the soul is found worthy,
it joins Umbernight as mist and myth,
immortal essence of the stories
of which it is woven.

If seen to be guilty
of The Sin of Mortal Mediocrity,
its memories are served up as blood,
its dying ember replanted in human womb,
just another wretched spirit
forever trapped
on the ghost train's tracks.

Vampire Wedding Planner

Promises written on melted ice,
whispered in forbidden tongue.
We cast our spell
on the ashes of witches,
script it in blood
from the executioner's axe.

    serpent's fang
    crow's quill
    bones from a pet cemetery
    all your mortal memories
    my apocalyptic kiss

Reception to follow
on the far shore of Styx.

GHOST TOWN

It's a nocturnal city
where old factories are castles,
where the street lights
are flowers of the night
whose blooms fall off
when the sun comes up,
where ghost towns are rejuvenated junk
piled by the side of the road,
masquerading as cities.
The hallucinations are willing
to play the game
if we can just stop fighting
what we think we know.
Is that me hovering outside the car
or just a reflection sucked pale
by the person I used to be?
We've passed the same truck three times
because I forgot to turn the clock back
when Nevada turned to yesterday
in the rearview mirror,
and I think Mother Earth slit her wrists
at the San Andreas fault.
That's what she told me
out here on the highway
while the day has given way
and the vampires are running
up and down these freeway veins,
looking for a ghost town called L.A.

Here the shadows have names:

    Wicker
    Twig
    Feral
    Cinders

Careful where you step.

AUDIENCE WITH THE KING

The King of Neverland is born of storms:
   red wine moonshine in his veins
   eyes of hurricanes
   lost ship driftwood bones
   tornado tempest tormented heart.
I met him once in the Mists of Missing Time.
Now the storm is all I (n)ever remember.

SEASON OF LEAVES

The clouds have come looking for you again
here at the intersection
of summer's end and autumn eve.
Lady Earth cloaks herself in grey,
pregnant with your storm-child
who waits for the thunder
to sing his birth,
the lightning to slash the womb
so he might find a way
onto this decaying stage.
I deck my room in cobwebs and masks,
hoping the season of leaves
will entice you from the mushroom's gills
where you have hidden,
waiting for this world to die.

DUALITY

Sliding through the gothic dark
on wings of karma and delirium,
the city is an old dream
of a place where men were temporal
and bones were planted like flowers
at the end of a short, sad season.
The nightmare comes daily
while evening returns me
to a land where time is trapped
inside the clock tower,
its hands tied together at midnight forever.
I wake into the dream
but dream myself awake,
raging at lines on the mirror
which deepen and crack
while I wail a mortal's immortal despair
at this peculiar duality
that keeps me always apart
from that eternal other self,
forever wandering phantom avenues
of perpetual gothic dark.

ACOLYTE

This winsome wind
is only the stray beliefs of the autumn king.
I kiss the restless air
to thank you for dreaming me real.
My throat bleeds—
food for your thoughts.

Goethe Passing By

It is a night when stars must fall
thru the fiery tears of their own cremation
and galaxies are committed to collide
because the universe isn't big enough
to hold them all,
and comets pass by
just to catch the lonely fragrance
of chimney smoke
swept on a wind so cold
it can't help but scream
as it drags its fingers
thru chimes made of old knives.
From the doorway of my haunted room,
I watch the world
spider-webbing herself alive,
and I know you're out there somewhere,
tip-toeing over the rooftops of mortals,
dancing with wolf shadows
and tipping your chimney-sweet hat
to the ghosts of a thousand dead poets
you have been
at one time or another.

REALITY INJECTION

Vampire sentinels stand watch
over the little pet cemetery
where my old familiars lie dead,
victims of time's treachery.
The chaparral drags her lace dress
over desert floor,
sweeping dust only to reveal more dust
while the coyote king cracks the midnight
with a dirge of mourning.
Dirty needles on saguaro fingertips
inject the sky with stars,
yet,
knowing her ultimate destiny,
would the night bird sing at all?

HOUSE GUEST

There's an archangel in my waterbed,
stygian wings folded
over iridescent flesh.
Tomorrow,
only the wrinkles on the pillow
will remain.
That,
and maybe a feather
shed in lieu of tears.

WAITING FOR THE PAIN

My heart is made of voodoo stuff:
      black magic wax
       and hair from your brush,
      shredded paper that once was poetry,
      mushroom stems for writing visions
      on the quantum fabric
      of time's fickle mind.
It lies still as death in my mortal chest,
waiting for the pain of you to waken it,
waiting for your blood to fill it,
waiting for eternity which has always been
to finally begin.

FRACTURED NIGHT

The footsteps of crickets
fall solemnly on shifting sands
and the wind is coming from a colder place
while voices clear as castrati
cry hymns of penance
into this fractured night.
An ebony-winged angel
lands in the clearing
to dance on star-cobbled stones:
      whisper of feathers;
      messages hidden
      in the paths taken by falling leaves;
      irregular rivulets of dry river beds
      where immortals come to drink
      unfulfilled human dreams.
Eternity flickers in the candle's last breath,
beginning where the light lapses,
where the darkness descends.

RITUAL

Each morning
I prick my finger,
leaving a drop of blood
in your tea cup.
When the vessel is full,
I will drink from it in your stead,
wishing you were here with me again.

GNOSIS

The wind in the garden blows indigo cold.
My heart is colder still.
Mortality's curse hangs over me,
Eve's legacy.
I summon the marrow of candles,
the gnosis of transcended sentience,
seeking solutions
beyond this horizon
of endless mausoleums.

CEMETERY WINTER

Soon I will whisper a white kiss
upon the unwed hand of Time
and turn the graves wrong side out,
hiding all the fallen cherubs
beneath my silent shroud.

Barnacles cling to the hull of *Titanic*,
silent observers of ghosts in black taffeta
who sip red wine
from fine crystal goblets
laid out on the ballroom floor
beneath the icy Atlantic.
Sometimes a vampire happens by,
out for an evening stroll
in a world where only the lost
have rite of passage.
Far distant,
a prisoner in the mortal continuum,
a crazy old crone
known to the mirror as myself
prowls the bleak autumn alleys of LA,
trespasser in Camelot of the Damned,
looking for the portal
to another time,
otherwhere, netherwhen.
A homeless man with whirlygig eyes
convulses fitfully in tormented visions,
crying out to unseen demons,
"It's in your head! That's where it's at!"
Dusk comes in shades of salmon,
pushing the sun
to the bottom of the ocean.
The portal opens,
a bony finger beckons.
In rush hour traffic,
the crone dances
on the bridge of *Titanic*.

CYCLE

Paintings on the surface of water
shivering stray energy
dreaming themselves solid.
Tree and acorn only constructs
woven together with frayed threads of time
tied together in the middle,
each already the other.
Robin's eggs sleep in tumbleweed nests,
waiting for feathers,
wings of birth,
already dust,
already death.

EARTHEN VESSEL

Night paints with black crayons
from a palette of shadows,
and the stars are pixie sprinkles
in the skeletal hand of time.
I look for evidence of immortals
and find only tombstones
worn thin as silk.
The mushrooms are singing hallucinations
and dreams are sneaking out of sleep,
lonesome ghosts
on the canvas of the No-thing.
I am the receptacle for this fragile world,
afraid of breaking
lest the contents spill
like fine dark wine,
wasted,
drying to dust.

WAITING FOR THE BEGINNING

I wanted to see you tonight
but you said there were a few things
you needed to take care of first:
    planning the pumpkin harvest
    and playing pinball with comets
    and lighting up all the constellations
    with an empty book of matches.
In a world without time,
when will there be time for us?

PROPS

She washes broken windows
in a house of ruins
haunted by her wanderling shadow.
A rice bowl sits untouched
on faded countertop,
just another prop
in a life of linear mirages.

FROM THE VEIN

I need to be drunk
on ambrosia of the damned,
vampire blood
straight from my maker's male breast.
The gods who made us mortal
weave idle braids of comet's tails
on crumbling stairways to heaven,
distant hints of their mocking laughter
fodder for my hottest hatred.
From Hell's basement
I cry to the graveyard of living souls,
yet the warning goes unheard,
echoing against tombstones and bones
settling in my own future crypt.
Hope and faith fracture,
fragile companions,
leaving only the steel blue certainty
of eternity.
From the vein of Lucifer's wing
I drink a toast
to all the fallen cathedrals,
to the truly cursed children—
mortals,
mortal still.

THE HARVEST

Moonbeams play over cluttered desk
where some naive past self
writes unpublished books
for me to read in decades hence.

The stereo glows blue,
painting Celtic tapestries
in an empty room
while the voodoo doll
I have become,
held together with glue
and paint and spent wax,
sits beneath the scarred stars,
pricking human consciousness
with a cheap Bic pen,
harvesting words like blood.

Time is a severed artery
from which the phantoms feed.

THE NEW & HOLY COVENANT

It's Good Friday
and all the icons are bleeding again,
porcelain eyes, crimson tears
for the misconceptions of pious men.
The holy grail is made of flesh
and resurrection is an evolution,
a congress of blood and visions
between man and vampire.

FOUNDATIONS

My fantasies have all burned away,
leaving only foundations
of dark magick imaginings.
Somewhere in the coyote hymn
lies the secret to life's meaning,
the antidote to reality,
the incantation to enter the dream.

ALTER-LIVES AND NETHER-SELVES

There's a ring around the moon,
   a round window left open
   from the place where owl song originates
   and dreams are steeped like rare tea
   too perfect to drink.
Under that portal,
   behind this curtain of stars,
   I glimmer thru gnostic visions,
   experiencing alter-lives and nether selves
   who exist a molecule to the left,
   a moment to the North,
   a breath separated from memory
   in an immortal trance
   where there is no thought of death.

SELF PORTRAIT

I Am...
    the vampire king's bad dream,
    mortal creature without wings,
    trapped in the trance
    of transient life.

WORRY STONES

There's a vampire playing marbles
    with acorns
just to pass the time
while kingdoms crumble
and gravestones rise and fall
and centuries pass
fleeting and bleak as fog.
Deep in the night
he courts the oaks with stories
of where the world has been,
where it might be going.
October brings the harvest,
acorns in frayed velvet pockets,
worry stones for immortal hands.

Leave It Be

Here it is forbidden
to sweep away the web-dwellers
or meddle in the dust.
These transient gypsies
remember our fatal destiny.

MYTHS

Myths escaped from grim little storybooks.
Mirrors deliberately shattered
    to free reflections and cold spots.
 Voices heard in vacant rooms
    and empty crypts
    where your shadow walks
    these lonesome catacombs
    somewhere in this nowhere night.

RUMORS OF VAMPIRES

Rain creates you,
a shadow on a side street,
shabby clothes snapping in the wind.
Unkempt,
you hide inside a song
blowing out through nightclub windows.
There's a bloodstain on the sidewalk
and rumors of vampires posing as men.

Dear Reader...

Thank you for looking at my humble book of attempted poetry. I hope you've enjoyed it and that perhaps it's brought you a smile or two or some tiny bit of insight into the heart of the lonesome vampire or the plight of the mortals who dream of him on cool autumn eves and darkest nights of the soul.

If you liked what you've read here, perhaps you'll consider leaving a good review on Amazon, since authors are dependent on reader reviews & reactions for sales, but more importantly, it's your interest and your kind words that provide the inspiration for the next project. And let's face it - in today's crazy world, we can all use some kindness and encouragement. Keep it going, and thank you for reading me!

Unconditionally, always,
Della Van Hise

About the Author...

Della Van Hise is a native of Florida, transplanted to California at the age of 21, who has subsequently sunk her roots into the desert near Joshua Tree National Park. She has not personally seen any aliens since around 1992, but there is rumored to be a secret UFO base underneath her house.

Della's writing started around age 11 on an old Smith Corona typewriter. No, not an electric one. A real antique, made of metal and heavier than a wet coffin. Her first professional novel was best-selling *Killing Time* - the controversial *Star Trek* novel which was recalled and re-edited in 1984 (making the first edition a rare collector's item) - and which was the foundational plot for the first *Star Trek* "Reboot" movie.

Della has written extensively in the non-fiction genre, with titles such as *Quantum Shaman* and *Scrawls On the Walls of the Soul*, *Into the Infinite*, and *Questions Along the Way*. If you enjoyed the works of Carlos Castaneda or Don Miguel Ruiz, you'll like the works of Della Van Hise.

In addition, Della has written professionally for Tomorrow Magazine and other prominent science fiction publications. Her most recent fiction works include *Sons of Neverland* (an award-winning vampire novel); *No Forwarding Address* (a science fiction quest of the heart's yearning); and *Coyote* (a young adult novel combining the mystical aspects of martial arts, coming of age, and personal sacrifice.) Della's other poetry books include *The Effect of Moonlight on Tombstones* and several chap books.

Della shares her life with her significant other, Wendy Rathbone, and a variety of cats, dogs and desert wildlife.

The Effect of Moonlight on Tombstones

A Dark Little Collection of Poetry Gleaned From the Gnosis of Vampires & Songs of the Muse

by Della Van Hise

Moments Frozen In Time
(A Foreword by the Author)

Poetry has never been something I consciously set out to write. Instead, it comes or not, entirely at the whim of whatever it is that writers call "the muse." Over the years, I have come to think of my poetry as a form of shorthand - an attempt to capture a moment frozen in time. A glimpse of a shadow cast by nothing at all. The effect of moonlight on tombstones.

Though I write primarily novels and nonfiction, I do find myself pleasantly haunted by what my mentor once referred to as "the gnosis of vampires." What does that mean? In essence, I would say it is the voice of silent knowing - the observer within all of us who possesses the ability to see the world clearly, and at times perhaps too clearly. As another dear friend once said, "Poetry is the streaming download from the broken heart of the universe." I have found that to be true, at least in my own humble attempts at the art form.

The poems in this anthology represent approximately two decades of those streaming downloads, most of which were scribbled hastily and in bad penmanship into cloth journals. If I have been at all successful in capturing some of those moments frozen in time, perhaps a line or two will resonate with you, hopefully bringing a smile to your face or a chill to your spine

At the very least, enjoy the dark side of the light.

SONS OF NEVERLAND
an erotic vampire novel
by Della Van Hise

"The virtuosity shown here is only the beginning of a pyrotechnic talent unfolding into the hidden dimensions of the human and nonhuman spirit."

-Jacqueline Lichtenberg

Set against a backdrop of contemporary culture, *Sons of Neverland* explores the universal questions of life & death, sex & love - the most crucial challenges every human being faces - through the eyes of the immortal vampire.

"What *Sons of Neverland* resembled to me was the creative hagiographies of Nikos Kazantzakis, where a few stylized characters deliver a message that goes way beyond the parameter of the characters themselves. And much like Kazantzakis, this book zones on the question of immortality. However, this is not just the decadent historical immortality of the long-lived vampire, it is immortality as a change in one's perception. This is the story behind the story, delivered by characters that are hyper-real - each one loaded with symbolism. *Sons of Neverland* will have you filled, even brimming over with the sense of Mysterium Tremendum et Fascinans. Go there for a full helping of the numinous." (A Reviewer on Amazon!)

Available on Amazon or directly from the publisher at
www.eyescrypublications.com

Prince of Umberlight
by Alexis Fegan Black

"If Prince of Umberlight doesn't rattle your cage, you're more dead than the undead!"
Night Readers

Thorn may be an 800 year old vampire, but he does not possess the ability to create others of his kind, and so he is cursed to fall in love with mortals, only to watch them grow old and die. Torn by grief, Thorn denounces his immortality and enters into a comatose oblivion for decades. When he awakens, he is no longer in London, but finds himself in a world spun into being by his own desires - a world where Time and Death do not exist, a world where it is forever autumn, where the Parish of Shadows and the River of Stars become his home. It is in this world of Umberlight that he meets Atom - an interloper into his private sanctuary, but also an impudent imp who is destined to reveal to Thorn the three dangerous elements a vampire must possess in order to become a Creator.

The Art of Brutality.
Submission to Dark Desire.
Love.

Available on Amazon or directly from the publisher at www.eyescrypublications.com

NO FORWARDING ADDRESS

A literary science fiction novel, *No Forwarding Address* explores the lures and the dangers of love, the tragedies and triumphs stirring in the human heart.

When Crystal and Raine first meet, it is 50 years after The Great War on Earth. They are hesitant to trust, afraid to love. But even if they overcome these seemingly insurmountable obstacles, is even love enough?

When a man has the stars in his eyes, legend says he must serve them above all others.

———————————

I knew then that it wasn't love and hate who were mirror twins. The final irony was that grief would always turn out to be the paradoxical antithesis and simultaneous manifestation of whatever it is that humans call love.

Crystal remained silent and walked a few steps away from Raine – further down the shoreline, until she stood under the wing of one fallen Phantom. She thought of the ship she had seen from the balcony of our home, and though it had long since disappeared over the dark and treacherous abyss of the ocean, its image lingered clearly in her thoughts. On that ship was a man, she thought. A terribly lonely man who made no great difference to the flow of time or the memory of the galaxy. A man who, like Raine, was compelled to keep moving and look only ahead and never behind. A man who could not afford the luxury of waving goodbye to friends on shore.

At last, she turned toward her beloved and watched him watching the darkness. He stood only a few feet away, yet the images in my mind said he might as well have been a million light years off in the void. He was lost to her in that instant out-of-time, just as lost and impossible to find as the light from that ship which had vanished over the horizon...

COYOTE
by Della Van Hise

When River Willows is accused of a murder she didn't commit, her life takes a turn toward the sanctuary of a world existing at right-angles to our own. Combining the mysticism of martial arts and the romantic conflict of a young woman torn between two powerful men, COYOTE takes the reader on an epic journey of dangerous secrets, military cover-ups, and the infinite heart of the peaceful warrior.

"So who's Coyote?" I asked, trying to ignore the effect he was having on me. "You?"

Steale laughed easily, though it did little to hide the torment behind that mask of indifference he wore so well.

"Coyote's a scavenger, Jack of all trades. The Native Americans call him the trickster - the one who brought chaos down on the world." He shrugged as if altogether unconcerned. "Original sin."

"Is that what you are?" I asked, keeping it light despite the growing knot my stomach. "Original sin?"

He kept his profile to me, eyes straight ahead as he drove. "Sure you want to know?"

I couldn't help wondering if I had cornered the coyote, or if the clever trickster had cornered me.

By the author of **KILLING TIME** – without a doubt the most controversial **STAR TREK** novel ever published!

Non-fiction titles from Eye Scry Publications...

TEACHINGS OF THE IMMORTALS
by Mikal Night

So... You Want To Live Forever?

The teachings are presented as brief vignettes in no particular order of importance. This is not a book you read from start to finish in a single night. It is a grimoire of self-creation, intended to be contemplated slowly so as to be assimilated wholly. Pick it up and turn to a page at random. Where your eyes come to rest on the page is your lesson for the day. Go no further until you have assimilated the lesson totally.

The teachings are seduction as much as instruction. This is the way of The Dark Evolution.

Perception

This is the nature of reality: to be precisely what perception dictates, as solid and whole as your interpretation of it, or as changeable and eternal as you permit it to be.

It wasn't knowledge god tried to keep from Man, you see. It was perception, for perception alone has the power to destroy god and obliterate comfortable consensual realities to create unending immortality.

Take the apple, my embryonic children. Nibble its red red flesh. Open your vampire eyes so you may finally begin to *See*.

www.immortalis-animus.com
or on Amazon

DARKER TEACHINGS OF THE IMMORTALS

MIKAL NYGHT

Teachings of the Immortals took the metaphysical world by storm, and now Mikal Night comes through on his promise to reveal the *"Darker Teachings of the Immortals"*.

Darker Teachings of the Immortals brings the reader into intimate contact with secrets that have been suppressed for centuries by governments, religions & corporations who seek to maintain a profitable status quo while simultaneously keeping the human population docile, obedient and - worst of all - mortal. Now, at last, it's time to throw off the chains and claim our rightful place among the immortals.

Listen with your heart.
Hear with your spirit.
See with your third eye.
Only then will you Know.

"*The Darker Teachings* will not only boggle the mind, they have the power to free it - and you - from the yoke of Death itself." (Night Readers)

"If you read *The Darker Teachings* before you're ready, you may end up holding a candlelight vigil for your sanity. An empowering look at the human potential!"
(Jonathan Abrahms, Independent Reviewer)

www.immortalis-animus.com

Quantum Shaman:
Diary of a Nagual Woman
by Della Van Hise

"Diary of a Nagual Woman picks up where Carlos Castaneda left off to take us on a roller coaster ride of our own forgotten power..." - Michael Grove

When I asked how Orlando had known I would come to this remote location, and how he himself had gotten there – since there were no other cars in the parking lot – he only smiled a little, stretched out his long legs, and slouched down on that cold metal bench to stare up at the stars.

"You're predictable," he said as if I should have already known. "I'm here because this is where you always come when you're mad at the world."

I attempted to engage him in a conversation of just exactly how he knew I was mad at the world but, he brushed my words aside with an easy gesture.

"Do you want to talk or do you want to waste time looking for logical explanations for every magical thing that ever happens?" he asked. "That's what's wrong with the world, you know. Instead of embracing the mysteries and trying to determine how they might open a crack in an otherwise humdrum, pre-programmed existence, people waste their entire lives explaining it all away, filing and categorizing it until it loses any meaning."

He had a point. He was *there* – whether physically or in some spirit-form is ultimately of no importance, for in the sorcerer's world there is no difference between body and spirit, and in any world, perception is reality.

www.quantumshaman.com

Questions Along the Way

Conversations With a Quantum Shaman
Della Van Hise

Anyone on a journey of personal growth is sure to come face to face with difficult questions that will keep them awake at night and may even plunge them into the dark night of the soul. In *Questions Along the Way*, Quantum Shaman Della Van Hise talks frankly with seekers on the path of heart and opens wide the door to a new understanding that lies beyond the false belief systems and cultural programming all of us must confront when emerging from the dark into the light.

Who am I? Where am I going? Is there a God? Are our lives predestined? Why am I here? Who *am* I?

The first and the last question are always the same. And somewhere in between lies the proving ground which we refer to with a simple 4-letter word known as 'Life.' Perhaps for many people these gnawing and persistent questions are nothing more than passing dalliances. But to anyone on a serious path of spiritual evolution, these questions form the basis for "the path with heart" - a term used by anthropologist Carlos Castaneda to describe the process of going from an ordinary human being to becoming a man or woman of Knowledge.

www.quantumshaman.com

Turn Left at November
Wendy Rathbone

Visit realms of diamond rain, dust-folk lands and valleys of curses and shame. Reside in the burning moonships of dream, the silt of stars, the asphyxiation of the waking day. Meet the golden android who houses your soul. Journey through tatters of stardust down roads of sorrow. Find hope in planets of candles and crazy-eyed mermen. There you will meet November in these rich and evocative poems by Wendy Rathbone.

Unmaking Autumn

Out at the excavation site
where they are taking apart autumn
leaf by fabled leaf
the searchlights try to catch us
putting the eyes back into the pumpkins
the moon back in the witch-shaped sky
We steal blood kisses
behind the naked apple orchards

Directly from the author:
www.eyescrypublications.com

Also on Amazon
or order from your favorite bookseller.

DEAD STARSHIPS
Wendy Rathbone

A collection of science fiction poetry by award-winning writer & poet, Wendy Rathbone. In the midnight realms of the deepest reaches of the stars you will find, floating gently and without apology, poems of long-lost thoughts made of dream and fantasy. This is where the poems in "Dead Starships" originate, from the endless, breathless muse that resides within us all and travels outward with abandon where every-day concerns fear to tread. Here you will find lost captains, alien princes, timeless androids, the sorrow, the longing, the nostalgia and the ecstasy of moving beyond the Earth and into the unknown. Open the pages of this book and set yourself on a voyage buoyed by the lullabies of the stars.

In the Future

the future comes with
too many gizmos
too many cute names that end in "i"
floating metal houses made for lightspeed
android lovers who can withstand
the heat of exploding suns
but cry at the thought of
a broken heart

Eye Scry Publications

A Visionary Publishing Company

www.eyescrypublications.com

Some of our authors include

Mikal Night
Della Van Hise
Wendy Rathbone
Alexis Fegan Black

www.ingramcontent.com/pod-product-compliance
Lightning Source LLC
Chambersburg PA
CBHW052148170626
46812CB00004B/1636